BECCI MURRAY

GRANNY'S EASTER EGGS ARE NOT THE SORT YOU EAT

A Granny Book

www.llamahousebooks.com

For Di Cantrell,
with love for being the first person
to read any of my books, ever

ISBN: 978-1-913944-30-8

Published by Llama House Children's Books

www.llamahousebooks.com

Granny had some treats inside her handbag.

Easter eggs for everyone today!

bag full of yummies

She took one out and passed it to my grandad,

But suddenly we heard poor Grandpa say....

1

There's a **LIZARD** in my Easter egg from Granny!

I almost chomped it like a tasty treat.

Your grandma might be grinning,

But this critter's eyes are spinning,

And this egg is not the sort that you can eat.

Granny passed the second egg to Mum.

I bet this one's got something good inside!

Mum's a proper egg-head

Mum took the egg and pulled the bow undone,
Then took a little nibble from the side....

6

There's a **TORTOISE** in my Easter egg from Granny!

I almost chomped it like a tasty treat.

I know it's just a nipper,

But it's chewing Grandpa's slipper,

And this egg is not the sort that you can eat.

Granny took a third egg from her purse.

I'm sure your dad's is better! she declared.

Dad's got a cockadoodle noodle

My father sighed, "It couldn't be much worse,"

Then bit the egg as quickly as he dared....

There's a GATOR in my Easter egg from Granny!

I almost chomped it like a tasty treat.

This croc is going dotty,

'Cause it wants to bite my botty,

And this egg is not the sort that you can eat.

11

Granny pulled a purple treat out next.

I'm pretty sure your auntie's egg's all right.

Auntie's feeling rosey today

Poor Auntie eyed it closely through her specs,

Then peeled away the foil and took a bite...

14

There's an **OSTRICH** in my Easter egg from Granny!

I almost chomped it like a tasty treat.

It's just a bird, of course,

But it's bigger than a horse,

And this egg is not the sort that you can eat.

Granny's largest Easter egg was pink.

I've got one for your uncle here as well.

Uncle's potty (but that's nothing new)

He tore off all the paper in a blink,

Then used a garden spade to break the shell...

17

There's a **DINO** in my Easter egg from Granny!

I almost chomped it like a tasty treat.

You really should've warned us

That I'd find a stegosaurus,

And this egg is not the sort that you can eat.

Everyone went

ABSOLUTELY

Mum's built a
deck-chair fort
to hide in

prehistoric
poo-shoe

prehistoric
poo-pile

20

CUCKOO!

And as the garden chairs were overthrown,

My uncle stepped in prehistoric doo-doo,

As Granny found an eggy of her own.

prehistoric
POO-machine

prehistoric
grandparents

21

Granny's
highly-suspiscious
face

22

I do not think I'll **BITE** this Easter eggy.

It might not be a very tasty treat.

It smells like choccy biscuits,

But I still don't think I'll risk it,

Just in case it's not the sort that you can eat.

SMACK!

She tried to whack it with a welly.

THUD!

She tried to break it on the floor.

BOING!

She bounced the egg off Uncle's belly.

24

SLAM!

She tried to crush it in the door.

ZING! She took a wand out of her pocket,

And tried to zap it with a magic spell.

Then - **BOOM!** - she tried to blast it with a rocket,

And finally a crack grew in its shell.

25

28

There's a **BUNNY RABBIT** in my Easter eggy!

He's brought us all a tasty little treat.

Now everybody's chummy,

'Cause there's chocolate in their tummies,

But....

COLLECT THEM ALL!

The hilarious series of gran-tastic catastrophes!

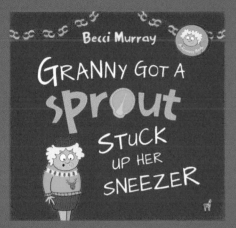
Becci Murray
GRANNY GOT A **sprout** STUCK UP HER SNEEZER

GRANNY DROPPED HER **chompers** DOWN THE TOILET

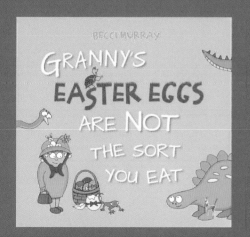
BECCI MURRAY
GRANNY'S EASTER EGGS ARE NOT THE SORT YOU EAT

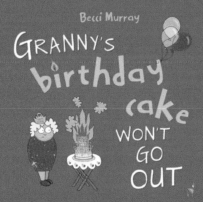
Becci Murray
GRANNY'S **birthday cake** WON'T GO OUT

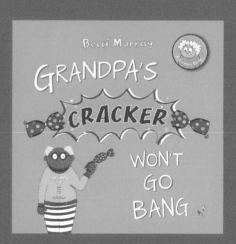
Becci Murray
GRANDPA'S **CRACKER** WON'T GO BANG

www.llamahousebooks.com

A fabulously fun rhyming read!

Becci Murray

Gerald Wants to Wear

PINK

FROM THE SAME AUTHOR

www.llamahousebooks.com

Becci Murray is a mum and proudly independent author from the UK. She previously wrote for children's television and is the creator of the best-selling 'Granny' book series.

If you enjoyed reading *Granny's Easter Eggs Are Not the Sort You Eat*, please consider leaving a review wherever you purchased the book to help other young readers discover the story.

Thank you for supporting an independent author.

www.llamahousebooks.com

you can see Becci's other books on her website

Printed in Great Britain
by Amazon

20555412R00022